AF407882

Escape from the Madhouse:

A Poetic Tale

Leon X

Author's Note:

I, the author, Leon X, do not promote any of these
actions done through this poetic tale, nor promote
any other actions expressed through any of my works
under Leon X, both in poetics and/or in novels.

Thank you for understanding.

- Leon X

Poetic Tale:

Meet Jac. Jac is imprisoned to a mental asylum based on a psychological profile done by a duo of a crooked psychologist and psychiatrist. They purposefully label him "mad" based on "normal societal behaviors" in their eyes. Little did they know that Jac was not only a legendary physicist but also a poet as well, whom he kept to himself.

Trapped inside the confines of a mental asylum based on an arrogant psychiatrist and psychologist label, Jac manages to survive day by day by speaking word to himself. He ponders on the idea of "mad" in the eyes of a power driven society he lives in.

Will it be enough to keep him alive for another day until enough petitions are signed to release Jac?

Only time will tell.

"Are we all not "Mad" in the eyes of the Lord?"
– Leon X

Jac

<u>**1**</u>
Is it Thy?
Or is it they?
Am Thy of mad?

<u>**2**</u>
Within the quadrants of fours,
Within the space of white?
And of steel?

<u>3</u>
And of photographs?
Or is it they that be of mad?
To think Thy am of mad?

<u>**4**</u>

Am Thy not a God?
Or of the Devil?
Am Thy of craze?

<u>**5**</u>

Is this the madness of God?!
Or of the Devil?!
ANSWER ME!

<u>6</u>
Whom hath curseth Thy?
Was it that witch?
Witch indeed?

<u>7</u>
Of that nasty order whom smell'th,
Thy should hath known,
Thy am not of the insane,

Thy am of the sane...
The thinking of over is to flood the meadows,
So Thy am to relax as a cloud over the blue hue,

<u>9</u>

Am Thy not of the Earth or is the Earth of Thy?
And Thy a'lone?
Am Thy not of the waters?

<u>**10**</u>
Or is the waters of Thy?
Am Thy not of creation?
Of the fires?

<u>**11**</u>

Must'th it be not?
Am Thy not of an Angel?
Are not the Angels made'th of fire?

<u>**12**</u>
And fires a'lone?
Of the dirt?
Is that not of Man?

<u>13</u>
And His inferior Wo'man?
And of pathetic child...
Is it true that Thy am of the mad?

<u>**14**</u>

Or of the sane?
Am Thy not great?
The greatest?

<u>**15**</u>
Am Thy not of Fire?
And of Ice?
And of Earth?

<u>**16**</u>

And of the ether before of Word?
Am Thy of the no sense to the invisible mind?
And only to speak of none,

<u>17</u>
Yet,
This madhouse is of fill'd,
With the many,

<u>**18**</u>
Yet,
Thy did of nothing?
Am Thy a fool?

<u>**19**</u>
Or of a wise man?
Only to be treated like a fool,
And of a nobody...

<u>**20**</u>
Up,
Up,
Up,

<u>**21**</u>

Into the Heavens or into the ether?
What is there to know'th after earth?
And the life sustained by only eating,

<u>**22**</u>
Sleeping,
And of breathing,
Is there not something a'more?

<u>**23**</u>
Of the yearn,
For the Heavens above?
And of its abode?

<u>**24**</u>
Or the art itself?
And its magnificence both in the seen,
And soon to be of the un'seen,

<u>**25**</u>

Are not cameras created for such?
Optics?
Physics?

<u>**26**</u>
To prove the unseen?
Or am Thy of folly w'unce more?
To sitteth here,

<u>**27**</u>
In the asylum of the mad,
A'lone,
For what?

<u>**28**</u>
Being Thyself?
Mad?
Whom is it to claimeth the mad?

<u>29</u>

Was it not the mad themselves?
Were they not mad themselves?
To knoweth of mad?

<u>**30**</u>
Or is it of their past,
They hath risen a'bove,
And now to diagnose?

<u>**31**</u>

Or am Thy of folly?

W'unce more as an idealistic mind in the clouds?

As to everyone in here is of folly?

<u>**32**</u>

Am Thy of God?
And He a'lone?
Only sent be'cause of the Truth,

<u>33</u>

That Thy am of Him?
And He a'lone?
O!

<u>**34**</u>

Only time will tell'th,
Thy hope not to loseth Thy mind within the walls of four,
As they all wish'th Thy do,

<u>**35**</u>

Only time will tell'th,
Yet...
Thy am neither contained by time nor second,

<u>**36**</u>
Nor day nor night,
Thy am beyond such mortal ways,
Thy am...

<u>**37**</u>
Thus,
Thy am to rest...
And be of peace,

<u>**38**</u>
Till the next breath of life,
Over the eons of forward progression,
Breath hath stay'ed the same,

<u>**39**</u>

As upon the last breath of the mortal flesh,
Am Thy not to go'eth?
Into the Heavens and Heavens a'lone,

<u>**40**</u>
And non'other,
So it be,
Thy am to rest...

<u>**41**</u>

Rest into the spaces of the ether,
Into the verses of the o'ther,
In between the dark and purple skies between worlds,

<u>**42**</u>

And only to be in peace,
And peace a'lone,
Regardless of the world of the physical a'round,

<u>**43**</u>

Thy am only in need of the body,
Mind,
And Thy...

<u>44</u>
Thy soul,
And soul a'lone...
They cannot containeth Thy soul,

<u>45</u>
Nor Thy mind,
Am Thy not in control?
As Thy wander into the eons of space,

<u>46</u>
Over the years of light,
As light itself,
Within this proclaimed "Madness",

<u>47</u>
And with'out,
Is not that of the universe?
Or am Thy of another folly?

<u>**48**</u>
So be it!
Of this house!
House of Mad,

<u>**49**</u>

House of Mad...
So they say'th...
Thy remain'th a'lone,

<u>**50**</u>
With Thy soul and of Thy mind,
Does not one need'th both to work'th magic?
Thy am only to ponder...

<u>51</u>

As Thy soon lay asleep and wunder the years of light
w'unce more,
Thy am only to pierce outside the windows of light,
As the mad be a'round,

<u>**52**</u>

And judge'th with their lack of thoughts,
And Thy am only to ponder w'unce more,
Into the realm of the unknown,

<u>**53**</u>

As a grain of light into another galaxy of star and of life
itself,
So it is to be'th,
Thy must'th be left of a'lone,

<u>**54**</u>

And a'lone it be'th,
Be'fore Thy am to sleep'th,
A question Thy am to ponder,

<u>55</u>

Within the confinement of this House of Mad...
Whom is it to be'th truly of the mad?
Thy?

<u>**56**</u>

Or of Thou?

Is not the Universe mad?

For those whom do not understand'th it?

End.

<u>About the Author</u>

Leon X is a novelist and poet.

Visit www.leonxtheauthor.com for more information on
the author.

Thank you for supporting.

<u>*Other Works by Leon X*</u>

Poetic Collections & Tales:

Limbs for Use

Wrath of I'Kan

Unlocking the Below

Disease Maker

Talking to the Mirror

Blood Coffee

Eye and Revenge

Sacrifice

Temple of Man

& More

Novels:

Disbelief

Comp-Passion

Gloom to Bloom

KALI